# Nymph

## Also by Francesca Lia Block

Weetzie Bat

Witch Baby

Cherokee Bat and The Goat Guys

Missing Angel Juan

Baby Be-Bop

The Hanged Man

Girl Goddess #9: Nine Stories

Dangerous Angels: The Weetzie Bat Books

I Was A Teenage Fairy

Violet and Claire

*the waters & the wild*

with Hillary Carlip
Zine Scene: The Do It Yourself Guide to Zines

4

# *Nymph*

*by*
*Francesca Lia Block*

**C+ Circlet Press**
Cambridge, MA

Printed in the United States of America
First Edition  June 2000
ISBN 1-885865-30-9

Circlet Press is distributed in the USA and Canada by the LPC Group, in the UK and Europe by Turnaround Ltd., and in Australia by Bulldog Books.

Circlet Press, Inc.
1770 Massachusetts Avenue #278
Cambridge, MA  02140
circlet-info@circlet.com
http://www.circlet.com

Alternative Cataloging-in-Publication Data
Block, Francesca Lia.

Nymph.

Cambridge, MA: Circlet Press, 2000.

9 short stories.

1. Short stories, American. 2. Erotic fiction. 3. Sexuality--Fiction.
4. Romantic love--Fiction. 5. Lovers--Fiction. 6. Love stories.

813.54--dc21

# CONTENTS

My intention is to tell of bodies changed
To different forms

—Ovid, Metamorphosis

# *Mer*

She rises up from the water, the drops slicking her breasts, beading tremulous at her nipples. The curve of her hips sheathed tight in something sheer and silver, glimmering beneath the narrow swoon of her waist. She tosses her head and smiles at him; her mouth is like the shadowy place nestled under the fabric that he knows he can never reach. He lumbers across the grasping sand toward the water, his cock leading him, plunging him into the wet salt swell.

When Tom Mac wakes he can still taste the waves and feel his limbs rocking; there is a silver-green light in his head and he has a massive hard-on. He knows there was more to the dream but he can't remember, and after a few minutes his erection is gone.

Maybe I'll go out today, he thinks but he knows he won't. It has been too long already. It will only remind him of how it had been before.

He gets out of bed to take a piss and sees his reflection in the mirror—sandy-blond longish hair and tan bristly skin, the lines around his blue-green eyes. His body has grown thick and slow, the once taut bulging muscles losing their tone. What would Tawny say if she saw him now? That she was right. Right for leaving. That she could have predicted this—the ex-pro living in the house now overgrown with wisteria vines, drinking too much, hanging out on the boardwalk, never touching his board.

Instead of going back to bed he tugs on the shirt that smells the least—a hooded woven one from Mexico, a pair of shorts and *huaraches*. His heart is thumping as if he really is going back to the water—he knows he isn't. But he also knows he has to get to the pier before the sun and the crowds. He has to get out there.

It is still early and gray and damp. A mist

hangs in the air, clings to his hair and skin, tasting of the ocean. Sometimes it is like fucking, he finds himself thinking for the first time in so long, when you ride the swell, feeling it folding around you glistening and wet and briney. And he can hardly remember either of them.

The boardwalk is almost empty. Later the vendors will arrive with their crystals and T-shirts and cheap sunglasses; the fortunetellers and clowns and acrobats will come, the bodybuilders and Rollerbladers and tourists. But now it is just Sage and Whitman and a few of the other homeless whose names no one seems to know, huddled on graffiti-scrawled wooden benches. Even the surfers haven't shown up; the sea looks flat and steely. The cans are brimming with junk food remnants, pigeons are scavenging; there is a slightly toxic smell. Tom thinks, And this is paradise, this is my paradise. Remembering Tawny dancing to the drums right here that night with her breasts straining the bikini top and the tyedyed sarong hanging low under her flat brown stomach. Her hair still crusted with salt and the way she always smelled like summer.

Tom buys five cups of coffee and distributes four to the men on the bench, keeps one, sips it even though it is still scalding, liking the feel of the burn on his tongue. Whitman says, "You up early, Mac," and Tom nods. Had a dream, he wants to say. They would probably understand. They aren't that much different than he is. Dreams, mostly forgotten, that keep you going when otherwise you might decide not to wake up again. And he is the lucky one, isn't he? Has the house to keep away the cold.

The house he'd bought at the height of things when he and Tawny first met, when he wanted a base in Southern California to return to between exotic wave-chasings. It is a small white Craftsman bungalow with a glassed-in porch, big windows; the wisteria vine with its purple blossoms has grown so thick now that not much light got in anymore. Tawny liked the wood floors bare and cool, the rooms mostly empty except for bed and pillows and boards. Now it is cluttered with shit and he keeps promising himself that he is going to do something about that.

Instead of going back he walks down the

boardwalk with his cup of coffee. He draws up his hood because the mist is forming drops now, but he doesn't want to go home. The dream is still whirling in the pit of his stomach, making his muscles twitch, scratching at his balls.

The girl in the wheelchair rides toward him out of the grayness. When he sees her Tom MacDougal feels as if he has swallowed a mouthful of salt water and it is caught in his throat. There are beautiful babes all the time, everywhere at the beach, but rarely this. So beautiful that he hardly notices the wheelchair or that her legs and feet are wrapped in tight silvery fabric covered with half-moon shaped spangles.

As she approaches him she smiles as if she knows him. Her teeth are white and sharp and her lips are stung, wet. He just keeps staring. Her eyes are crystally green and wide-spaced. Her breasts show through her soaking T-shirt, every curve and swell and the tender dark nipples so he feels as if he is touching them. Then she runs her long slender fingers over her collarbone, the slope of breasts, lingering beneath them and pulls the T-shirt off. Rain spills in rivulets over her perfect brown body. Perfect, he thinks, she is perfect.

Crazy perfect, like him, alone in the rain, pulling off her shirt for a stranger.

He approaches her slowly, the way you would a startled animal, although she doesn't seem afraid. His voice is hoarse and soft. "You okay?"

She nods, still smiling at him. He tries not to stare at her breasts. They seem too big for her delicate frame, her waist so small and her ribs showing. "You'll get cold, sweetheart."

She shakes her head, swinging the matted blonde dreadlocks that hang down to her waist.

"Do you need some help?" he asks her.

She gestures for him to come close. He can feel his cock stirring in his shorts. Smelling her; she is clean, salty. He wants to dive. Her nipples are erect; he wants to feel them against his lips. Everything tingling.

She reaches up and touches the side of his unshaven face with her finger, letting it slide down over his adam's apple. "Take me home with you," she says softly.

The whole impact of the night before is back, his penis throbbing. He takes off the woven shirt and gives it to her. "Put this on. You'll get sick."

She pouts slightly like a little girl but does it, getting caught so that he has to help her, trying to avoid touching her breasts. Her head emerges through the neck hole of the shirt, those eyes and that sly sweet mouth so close to him, that wild hair. "Take me home, Mac."

He figures one of the guys at the beach has told her his name. But still it startles him. And he wants to know.

Tom wheels the girl back up the boardwalk across the street to the house. He leaves the wheelchair at the foot of the porch and takes her in his arms. She is very light but also longer than she looks in the chair. Her lower body feels much more muscular than he would have thought, the tight weight of her ass against his forearms and wrists. Her long slender arms circle his neck the way a child holds on. He feels something like power returning to him, like right before he used to take a wave.

"This is a pretty house," she says, staring at the purple blossoms that have grown over everything. "It's like being under water."

Sometimes I wish it was, he feels like saying. He puts her down gently on the torn couch, then goes to get her chair.

"Do you want to take a bath? I can give you a pair of pants." She laughs and shakes her head. "What about coffee? Or I think there's a can of soup somewhere."

She makes a little face and laughs again. "You look different," she says.

He squints at her.

"We've met? I think I'd have remembered you, sweetheart."

"It was a long time ago, Mac." She adds matter-of-factly, "You were unconscious."

Tom sits beside her on the sprung sofa. She plays with her hair, pulling the heavy knotty strands up off her face. She has very high cheekbones and a small firm chin which makes her lips look even fuller. "What's your name?" Tom asks.

"Mer."

He shakes his head.

"Do you want to fill me in here, darling?"

Instead she smiles again and pulls his shirt off of her. She lifts her hands to her hair again so her breasts rise. The aureoles are big and dark. He wants to hide his hard cock. She takes his tense hands in hers and presses them against her breasts. An electric shock goes through him at their breadth and smooth fullness. They feel soft and heavy and almost buzzing with sensation. She throws her head back and moans roughly as he fingers her nipples. Her whole body shudders and she takes his head and gently draws him to her left breast; his tongue circles the nipple and her body is shaking more now. She leans closer to him, pressing her big succulent mouth to his neck. His breath comes in gasps and his heart pounds as if he is drowning. She moves over his rough, bare, sun-darkened chest with her lips. His cock feels huge, full of ocean.

"Who are you?"

She keeps going, looking up at him sometimes, smiling with those sharp white teeth that could tear; he gently touches the back of her head, the tender nape of her neck, stroking her. Her spine looks fluid and fragile. She undoes his shorts slowly, softly, her nimble fingers sliding the zipper down carefully to avoid his erection. Then he's out, big in her hand. Holding him she slithers back up and runs her tongue over his mouth, parting his lips with hers, sliding her tongue into him. The salt taste of his dream. He jolts up feeling her fingers move on his cock. She goes down again, this time her mouth on him, taking him in all in one slide so that he feels the back of her throat.

While she licks and sucks, her lips cupping the tender head of his penis and then swallowing him to the balls, Tom is remembering the dream. That time when he had the accident. What really happened. The waves pulling him down down. No air. Just this endless shining blue that he didn't really want to leave. He could have stayed there. He could have stayed. But then something was holding him; he knew he was safe. Rocking him like a baby. And her strong slender body carrying him back to the light, to the air. Because you belong here, she told him. I can't keep you. Even though you are the most beautiful of all of them. And you know my ocean more than any of them will ever know it. Tom moves with her, his groin spasming, his cock driving farther into her wetness. Suddenly there is that feeling in his balls. He doesn't want it yet but it is too much, he feels his whole body waking from some long sleep, as if he has been under water this whole time and only now has she rescued him. He gasps for air as he breaks through the surface, his semen spurting out in milky bursts that she swallows, his cock still hard for a long time after, still coming into her lush mouth.

Mer stays with Tom MacDougal in the little beach house with the wisteria vine and the glass porch. No one knows what goes on in there, only that Mac has started surfing again, every day, up at dawn with the kids, taking the big waves, ferocious and fearless as he had been ten years ago. And that his mysterious young girlfriend in the wheelchair sits on the sand and watches him, that when he returns from the sea he plunges to his knees before her and kisses her as if she contains the breath he had lost that time he almost drowned. Maybe she does. People speculate as to how they fuck, what is under the narrow spangled sheath she always wears over her lower body. Some think she is crazy, playing out a fantasy so

he can't get inside her. Maybe she'd been molest-
ed as a child or raped as a teenager travelling
along the coast and that is why she invented the
wheelchair thing and the costume. Others think it
is real. But Mac and Mer don't care. His mouth on
her tender, swollen, glossy breasts making her
come when he caresses her nipples; her mouth
sliding down the shaft of his thick cock, they rescue each other from land and from the sea again
and again.

# *Spirit*

Sylvie wishes the anti-depressants had been around when she was in her early twenties, not only to rescue her from the dark tunnels that came when her brother first got sick, but also to keep her from fucking all those assholes. There was the nightmare-plagued football player who punched her in the stomach while they were both sleeping and the skin head who only showed her his swastika tattoo after he'd come inside her. She thought meeting Ben would take her out of the tunnels but it didn't. When he is holding her, when he's firm up inside of her like a promise, she feels completely safe; it is the rest of the time that is the problem. And then her shrink recommended the drug.

So she isn't depressed anymore but she doesn't want to make love either. And after awhile it affects Ben, too. He starts spending more time at work and they both are reading the paper through meals or watching TV at night. She knows he isn't going to tell her he doesn't like what the medication is doing; the tunnels are at least as hard on him.

The house has been hidden behind a hedge for as long as they've lived in the apartment across the street and the same day the foliage is cut down the construction company sign goes up. Ben and Sylvie are walking down to Main Street for coffee and bagels when they see it. She doesn't notice the sign, just the house. When she'd first gone on the drugs there was an advertisement for them with a picture of a sunny white cottage with blue sky showing through all the windows and doves flying around the chimney and so she imagined the end of her depression would be like that, like a light, pretty house and no more dark tunnels. The end of her depression was more like nothing, like a vague calm in which she could move her limbs with a certain amount of ease and in which she could sleep and eat and get through each day the way other people seemed to. But this is the house she had imagined and it has been across the street this whole time, hidden behind the hedge, with its sloping green roof and glassed-in green house porch and the carving over the windows, the little garden now gone to seed and the braided wisteria vine covered with purple flowers overgrowing everything.

Ben notices the sign and says, "It's a crime what they're doing with all these nook and cranny type places. I mean we didn't even know it was here and now it's probably going to be gone over night and some hideous condo..."

She stops and looks at him and she knows that in the past her eyes would have filled with tears and the hollow blackness would have opened up inside her chest, but instead she just thinks, I am sad about this, this is a sad thing, and then she and Ben turn away from the house and go down to Main street and get their bagels and coffee and read the paper while they eat and drink and don't hold hands on the way home the way they used to.

But that night Sylvie can't sleep thinking about the house. It is the house she and Ben had always wanted. Whenever they saw the little beach bungalows with the wind chimes and the flowers and the surfboards on the porch, they'd stop and talk about how great it would be when they could move out of the apartment, how there would be a garden of jasmine and honeysuckle, space for a puppy and a baby's room. They both like the same ones—a little run down, maybe the paint peeling in places from the damp air, but always those porches and big windows and gardens. When they'd first met Ben took her on a walk on the beach and then they'd come back through the neighborhood and he'd stopped her in front of the grass-green and white cottage covered in morning glories and pressed her to him, so she felt his full, slightly chapped lips and then his tongue caressing her like it was lapping between her legs and his cock in the soft khaki pants against her almost bare pussy under the little slip dress and she knew they'd make love that night and the depression would be gone.

Sylvie turns to Ben who is reading with his

back to her and she touches his shoulder. He winces a little and then keeps reading for a second and then he turns back around. It used to be that the slightest touch would bring him to her; she had loved how in the night sometimes her hands would move as if on their own to feel the hard bunch of his bicep or the flat ridge of his abdomen or to find his cock and how he would respond right away as if he'd been waiting for her in his sleep, getting hard, pulling off his boxers, wrapping her up and pulling her onto him as if he'd been waiting.

"What?" he says, taking off his little rectangular glasses, squinting at her.

"I wanted to go see that house."

"Go see it? They're tearing it down, Sylv."

"I know they are. That's why. I want to go sleep there tonight."

He puts his glasses back on and sits up.

"What are you talking about."

"I just wanted to. I don't know. I wanted to go there."

She gets up and puts on her jeans; she always wears panties and a T-shirt to bed now—then steps into her flip-flops. He sits watching her. It is a warm night; she won't need a jacket. She thinks about putting on a bra but she doesn't feel like taking the time to go into the other room or letting him see her breasts right now.

Ben is looking at her like she has completely lost it but he doesn't say no. He gets up too and dresses and they go out into the night that smells of sea and flowering vines. The house has a weird almost phosphorescent glow and it is tinkling; there are some old glass shell-shaped wind chimes hanging from the porch.

"They've probably been there for thirty years," Ben says.

Sylvie nods. She wonders what would happen to the chimes. She can't imagine they are really going to tear this place down. What about the bevelled glass and carved wood and the wisteria vine? What about the spirits, she is wondering. What will happen to the spirits of the people who lived here before? Then she has a chill as if she is standing naked there all of a sudden, in front of the eyes of the house, and she hugs herself, rubbing away goosebumps even though it is a rare warm night.

"You cold, baby?" Ben asks and it startles her; he hasn't called her that in a long time. "Want my jacket?"

"I'm okay."

"I can't believe you really want to go in. We could get busted."

The wind chimes tinkle and the glow from the house seems to brighten as if some center were alive and burning. Sylvie thinks, they were beach people who lived here, they were sea people, they made love like the ocean.

She reaches out and takes Ben's hand and leads him through the hole in the gate, past the No Trespassing sign. No trespassing. What the hell did the people who were tearing this down think they were doing to the spirits? Stomping out. Destroying.

They creep up the creaky steps and across the porch. Cracked, weed-filled flowerpots are clustered against the green glass. It had been like an arboretum, steamy with the breath of flowers. The front door is unlocked; someone must've figured it didn't matter since the whole thing was coming down so soon anyway.

Their shadows stretch on the wooden floors and they just stand there for a long time, listening to the wind chimes and the sea and an occaisonal car.

"I feel something," Sylvie says. She touches her belly. There is a low scratching like a little hand. Ben walks away and she follows him into the kitchen. When he turns to her his eyes are flashing and he looks different, almost wild or sick with fever.

"I think whoever lived here were really in love," Sylvie says, turning away from him and touching the shredded lace hanging from the window. "I think they were insanely in love and they died here together."

Ben comes up behind her and she feels his breath on the naked nape of her neck. "He was a surfer," he says. "He found her on the beach. She came out of the sea." His hands grasp her elbows and he presses his crotch against her ass. She feels his cock between her cheeks. "They couldn't make love the regular way," he whispers. "Because she wasn't a regular girl. But it didn't matter. They made love all the time anyway. It was the only time they felt safe. She never went back where she came from."

*La mere,* Sylvie thinks. What if I couldn't ever feel him inside me again? Suddenly she is drenched, the wetness soaking through her panties. She has these long legs that she can spread wide for Ben. This soft wetness between them. She turns to face him and they stare at each other in the strange light that makes their eyes glow as if they are underwater.

Ben keeps staring into her eyes as his hands grab her waist, then move up to her ribcage holding her as if he could crush the fragile bones. His fingertips trace the bottom of her breasts and she throws her head back as he moves up over the tender nipples. Sylvie thinks, what if I couldn't ever feel him again between my legs? My breasts would get so sensitive. My nipples would be like clits. He pulls off her T-shirt and lifts her onto the sink. Her legs wrap around his narrow hips and she pulls him between her thighs feeling his hard chest against her fullness. The lips of her pussy are swollen, her clit standing up against the fabric of her panties and the hard buttons of her Levi's. His hand goes down there, grabbing at her fly, unbuttoning her and fumbling with the lace panties. He tugs on them so that they form a little hammock for her clit and she starts to breathe so hard she thinks she is drowning.

Ben carries her into the other room, what must have once been the bedroom, tosses down his jacket and lies her gently on it. Then he slips off her sandals and pulls off her jeans.

Sylvie spreads out her arms and legs, dipping her hands into her panties, pulling them off her hips to show him, then hiding in them again. "Do you want to see, baby, you want to smell, you want to taste. Mmm it tastes good. You want to touch." Things she's never said before. Like she's possessed by someone who is doing this for the first time, after years and years of waiting and wanting. He grabs her hands and holds her panties away so he can see. He puts his nose inside and rubs it against her. He runs his tongue over her in one lick and then he yanks off her panties and spreads her thighs apart. Then Ben pulls off his shirt and his jeans. His cock is straining in his boxers. She wants him to crush her. She rocks him in her arms and with her pelvis feeling the weight of his cock. Gasping as Ben lifts her onto him and flips over so he is on his back. She straddles him and he takes her left breast in his mouth. He closes his eyes and starts sucking. She pulls away and he grabs it back. She keeps pulling and he keeps reaching. She lets her breasts fall heavily against his delicate face. The erect nipples graze his lips. He lifts his head to get them but she keeps lifting herself away. Then Sylvie falls down on him, drowning him in the flesh of her breasts. She hears him make a soft moan almost as if something hurts him. She moves her hips down a little and feels his cock lying on his belly between her legs. Her heart is beating so fast and her wetness is drenching them both.

Sylvie whispers, "I don't have my diaphragm."

"It's okay," he says. "It will be okay, baby. We're going to be together."

She lifts her hips, hovering them above him and then all of a sudden in one plunging thrusting suction motion, he's inside. But also it feels like she is inside of him. Can't tell the difference.

His big thick cock is hers and her tight wet pussy is his. She starts coming right away in that deep convulsive way like when you feel your whole body will turn itself inside out, your heart exposed. It goes on and on in throbbing waves. Crouching over him, coming and coming, feeling his cock in her heart, in her throat and deep between her thighs where she has been closed for so long. When Ben comes he bucks so hard that she feels her ass almost tearing and his cock driving deep against the wall of her still-contracting sex. He just keeps saying thank you over and over again, thank you baby. He falls asleep on her breast almost right away.

They wake a few hours later and help each other dress as if they are children, then walk quietly through the house. Good-bye, Sylvie tells the spirits. Thank you. Ben takes down the shell-shaped wind chimes and hangs them around her neck like a necklace from beneath the sea.

The next day he has to go to work and Sylvie watches the demolition alone. The foreman keeps giving her dirty looks; he must feel guilty, she tells herself, he doesn't want to be doing this, it's his job. In the past he would have driven her away like that. But she wants to see everything--the delicate roof and walls caving in like a wedding cake, the windows smashed like sugar, the wisteria vine crushed like frosting flowers Maybe the spirits will escape inside of her. She hasn't taken her medication and she cries for hours. Not safe, but she is alive in her wind chime necklace. That night Ben comes inside her. And she is both.

# *Milk*

She isn't sure why this thing happens. She sees them there and she feels something come alive in her chest that then becomes indistinguishable from the feeling between her legs. It's in how they look at her, how they let her touch them; at first she thinks it is about their need but then realizes it is more about her own. This makes her try to stop, and she does stop for awhile, tries to convince herself to start seeing Thomas, the young intern who won't stop calling. They have one date but he seems so preoccupied, doesn't seem to want to hear about her life much at all, wants to talk about his job and how beautiful she is.

She always tests them this way: does she feel she can tell them about Kevin. Usually the answer is no. With Thomas it's no.

Then David comes and she forgets what she's been trying not to do. He is different from the others. He is only twenty for one thing, and beautiful. His sister, Sylvie, wants her to know how beautiful. She brings photographs of David before he was sick. Thick dark hair falling into his eyes. Tan lean muscled runner's body. Laughter—white teeth. His sister wants the nurses to know who they are dealing with—saving, maybe. The sister thinks it will help stir their compassion—he's not just another skinny bald dying person. None of the patients were before this. David was an athlete, an honor student, studying to be an architect; in the pictures he is playing with puppies and little kids, he is always smiling, he is so healthy looking it is shocking to see him now. But Nurse Milk isn't shocked the way others are—his friends and family. She sees his beauty just as much—his sister didn't need to bring the pictures. He has lovely bones and eyes and hands and she sits with him all night sometimes, whispering about dogs and music and movies and what would be a perfect date. They have the same taste—golden retrievers, early Cat Stevens and Joni Mitchell, *Harold and Maude*, dinner at the cantina on the coast and sleeping at the beach. He looks at her with his dark huge eyes that seem like they've seen everything for a few life times and she knows he's falling in love with her—not like she hasn't seen it before. Somehow, though, this is different. She gets scared and asks about his girlfriends—there are lots of young women in the pictures. He laughs and asks her how many she's ever seen around there.

"They're just afraid," she tells him, and adds so he won't misunderstand, hear the words of you dying in his head, "Of acting the right way."

He stares at the side of her face. "Where'd you get so tan?"

She tells him, "The beach."

"Was it a good date?"

"Date? No I just went with Rudy." Her golden retriever.

"I can't believe that. You're the most beautiful woman I've ever seen."

She has to go then; it's too much. Maybe he does need her too, she thinks.

As a little girl after her brother Kevin died in the car accident, she nursed sick animals—fed broken baby birds with bottles, wiped away discharge from the eyes of stray kittens, cooked special meals for sick dogs. Later she started making up games with the boys; never Doctor—she always got to examine them. They let her. She had white blonde hair then. It is a little darker now. She got breasts early. Sometimes if she really liked the boy she'd hike up her skirt and let him touch her thighs while she took out his penis.

She thinks of David again at night in her bed. He's not going to die, she prays. Don't let him die. He's only twenty. He's only twenty.

She feels guilty, tries to justify her desire. He's a man—he's had lots of girlfriends, well not lots but some, and what if what if there isn't much time—don't think that, Karen—but what if it it helps him recover?

His sister comes the next day and they talk. The sister tells her how much David likes her—how he can't stop talking about her. Almost sounds like she's trying to set up a date, Karen Milk thinks. She ends up comforting the sister, Sylvie, saying he'll have a chance to be with all those old girlfriends again really soon.

The next night Karen Milk goes to him. He's lying in bed with his hand in his shorts. He moves it quickly but he doesn't avert his eyes from her face.

"I'm sorry," she says.

"No. I knew you'd be coming now. I'm sorry."

"It's fine, David."

She goes over to him and checks the chart at the foot of his bed.

"Not that this is much good anyway," he says, meaning his cock. Resigned. Never sorry for himself. Just matter of fact. She wants to touch him so badly it feels like she's the sick one—trying to hold on to something alive. She feels a trickle of moisture in her panties; they're too skimpy to absorb much.

"Would you like some water?"

He nods and she hands him the cold cup which he gulps down.

"Are you going to examine me now?" he asks. His voice is more like a growl.

"Do you want me to?"

"Please." From deep in his throat.

She sits beside him and lets her fingers rest lightly on the sheet. He stares at her face. She feels his eyes like hot lights on her cheek and throat and down between her breasts where a trickle of sweat slithers toward her belly. She slips her hand under the sheet and massages the muscles in his thighs.

"I can tell you're a runner."

"Was."

Her hand inches up towards his groin, fingers graze his scrotum. She thinks there are tears in his eyes.

"I haven't come in months," he says. "I can't even get hard."

"It's time for your meds," she whispers.

His pupils look on fire. She climbs onto the bed. She's wearing a garter belt and white stockings, a white satin bra and the tiny panties under the uniform. The panties are pretty useless though. Her pussy so wet with hardly anything to absorb it. She climbs onto his chest, soaking him. Tugs her breasts out of the bra so they spill into his mouth and he sucks and sucks until they are bruised and she is stifling cries and then she crawls up over him so her pussy is just above his lips, pulls the tiny strip of fabric to one side and she says, "You need your other meds now, David." He reaches with his tongue, like he is really thirsty, like he is begging for it, his eyes closed, his eyelids fluttering, his mouth quivering and she lowers and lifts her body so his tongue grazes her clit which is swelling and he is trying to drink from her dripping body but she keeps moving away and finally smashes down and he's tonguing her lips and rocking her clit around and she manages to reach around and take his hands and put them around his hard cock and he starts stroking it while he's still kissing her pussy and sucking her clit and she feels him stroke up and down hard and fast hard and fast while she's falling onto his mouth and he moans into her with his whole soul calling into her as the hot cum bursts up the shaft and out the sweet mild tip and shoots out like relief, like love, like Nurse Milk's tears.

～

She's off for a few days after that. She goes to the beach with Rudy and runs on the sand, tries to smile back at the healthy, tan men that smile at her. She reads some fashion magazines and finishes a novel and calls friends and buys new underwear. When she's back at the hospital she goes into David's room to tell him this can't happen again until he gets out. Then if he wants to... but then he'll probably have so many girlfriends he'll forget about her. She is planning just what to say so that he'll feel okay about it and so that she will, too. Doesn't want to let him go yet. He kissed her with more life than any of the healthy guys she'd ever been with. Remembering how Thomas kissed on that one date. Like he had all the time in the world and nothing mattered that much. Before she left him, David kissed her like it was all that mattered.

So how could it be? How could he be gone. She's not cut out for this work. Maybe I should be a prostitute, she wants to scream, Johns don't die on you and you make them feel better. My God,

David. She knows it metastasizes faster in young people sometimes. But this is too fast. She finds one of the pictures of him before he was sick. Sylvie, left it for her. Karen wants to tell her, "I lost a brother, too," but she knows it won't help at all. Nothing will. What helped her? Time. Taking care of the little sick animals. Making love to the patients. It's been thirteen years, she thinks. A lot of the animals died. Some of the patients, too. David. Nothing's helped much.

"Thank you, you really helped him. He told me you were a miracle worker," the sister wrote on the back of the picture.

If only.

That night she goes home and calls Thomas. When he hears her sobbing, he's over there in moments, taking her in his arms.

"What's wrong, Karen? What happened?"

He studies her face with a look she's never seen from him. Instead of David she tells him about Kevin. Expects him to say it was a long time ago, Karen. Why is it hitting you now? Maybe you should seek some professional help.

He doesn't say anything like that, just holds her.

"Pretend you are dying," she says to him. "Please. And make love to me like that."

His kisses get harder, deeper, he's plummeting into her, breaking her open, her thighs feel like they're tearing. "Something is different," he sobs when he comes.

It's too soon, she thinks. But Thomas is alive now, whispering over and over again that she is his miracle.

That word again.

# *Milagro*

From the time she is very young, all Plum wants is this: to be loved for who she is with complete and awesome devotion. She tries to dress herself the way she feels inside so that the love of her life will recognize her easily. Which means that in elementary school she wears as many barrettes as she can fit in her long black hair and shortens her skirts daily, letting them down again before her mother sees. In junior high she staples rhinestone studs to her clothes. In high school she chops off all her hair, to her mother's horror, and spikes it with gel. She designs clothes covered with zippers and chains and does her eyelids like various flowers and insects—orchids, dragonflies.

This is when she meets Santiago. He recognizes her by her radical hair and the clothes she has designed and made. Her soft voice and delicate hands and the way she comforts him when he calls to tell her about how his father tried to beat him again.

Santiago wears make-up and jewelry. He is so beautiful that no one except his father gives him shit. Everyone is infatuated with him, whether they know it or not—the popular girls, the shy girls, the jocks, the gay boys. Plum is the one who gets him. He is all she wants. She gives him haircuts and does his eyeshadow. He looks like a supermodel. They take ballroom dance lessons and go to punk gigs and do the tango in the pit. They are so charismatic together that instead of being shunned because of how eccentric they are, they are elected "Cutest Couple" in the yearbook. Plum realizes that this means everyone thinks they are sleeping together, and that maybe that is another reason why Santiago doesn't suffer (except from his father) because of his appearance. She also wishes that it were true—the sleeping together. They have never even kissed although they hold hands and when they are dancing, pressed up against each other, hearts slamming—it is like what she imagines it would be like to make love.

They go to the prom together wearing matching black zippered satin and leopard prints and boots and sporting matching bleached blond hairdos that contrast with their dark features. They do their punk tango and sit at the table with all the "Class Bests." They feel like rock stars. Plum realizes that she is in love with Santiago when he feeds her dessert with a spoon and tells her that he is not going to go back east to school the way he had planned because she is so beautiful.

After the prom they get in Santiago's old Cadillac and drive to the desert. On the drive they listen to their favorite B-52's tapes really loud, open the windows so the warm winds lash their faces, and scream into the night like banshees. Plum feeds Santiago grapes and chocolates as they speed down the highway.

In Palm Desert there are natural hot springs running under the desert floor. The motels were built around them over the years. There are little mom-and-pop places decorated in blond wood where Swedish moms and pops give deep tissue massages, pink and turquoise 50's style places, fake Roman set-ups with bad replicas of David and Venus around the pool, and broken down deserted bungalows that seem haunted by lost desert ghosts when the sand blows through. Then there is Villa Milagro. The pale blue bungalows surround a mosaic tiled pool and a glassed-in jacuzzi. There are large chunks of crystal and candles and garden shrines and silk flowers in the garden.

When Plum and Santiago get there in the still, hot, coral-colored desert dawn, Milagro, wearing beads and a long caftan decorated with birds, checks them in. Plum can't tell if Milagro is male or female. Milagro says, "What a beautiful couple you are." Plum and Santiago are shown to their bungalow decorated in Chia pets, clown paintings, beaded curtains, glass baubles, fabric printed with ferns and daisies, strands of fake roses and throw rugs covered in sunflower designs. It is fresh and smells like clean desert air. They collapse on the butterfly-adorned comforter and fall asleep almost right away. They sleep straight through till the next evening.

When she gets up, Plum goes to find Milagro. Milagro is sitting by the pool wearing a caftan decorated with ladybugs. Plum asks where they can get some food and Milagro takes Plum into Milagro's bungalow which is afire with glass objects refracting the light. Milagro prepares avocado sandwiches and fresh figs.

Milagro stares at Plum silently until Plum winces.

"You have a gift," Milagro says.

Plum thinks Milagro is talking about how she designs clothes and applies make-up but she realizes that she is only wearing her bathing suit and her face is bare.

"The love gift," Milagro says.

Plum feels shivery and assumes it's from the swamp cooler blasting rosewater scented air at her neck. The love gift. Does this mean she has found her love? She thanks Milagro for the food and says she has to get back to Santiago.

He is sitting on the bed wearing his swim trunks. His rippling deep amber colored body is even more glowing in desert light He grins at her.

The sky is pink with sunset, a neon motel sign flashing in the distance, a cluster of palm trees, otherwise just desert everywhere around the pool. The air warm and sparkling. They put their feet in the soft glow of blue water and eat the avocado sandwiches and figs. The sky changes to blue-violet and a crescent moon comes out with her stars.

Plum tosses the towel away. "Are you going to swim with me?"

She jumps in the water. It slides over her body like a warm slip of silk. She floats and splashes, looking up at the glint of moon and smelling the burnished sweetness of the desert night.

"What's that smell?"

"Creosote."

"It smells like rain."

He dives in. The water ripples out from the force of his body. She feels it rush against her abdomen, forcing her bikini bottoms away from her pelvis. A current rushes between her legs. They swim around and then Plum slips through the little entrance into the glass Jacuzzi.

Santiago comes in after her. In their own private cave of steam. Milagro has lit some candles along the outside rim and the crystals are throbbing in their light. There is also incense that has a light scent of vanilla and exotic flowers. A collection of mermaid statues are poised ready to splash into the water. Plum presses back against the lowest jet. She is afraid to turn around because if the jets hit between her legs she thinks she might start coming. It's being around him and seeing his bare chest and it's the heat and the air and the sky. Santiago lies back and closes his eyes. The water stutters against Plum's tail bone. Between that and seeing Santiago lying there with his brown arms floating above the ripples of water she thinks she might come even without turning around. She moves closer to him.

He says, "You look like a mermaid."

He switches places with her so his body is up against the low jet.

She says, "Give me my jet."

He laughs. "I don't have your jet."

"Yes you do!"

She wants to reach out and stroke him under the water.

Later, in the kitsch paradise, their bodies still whir with heat from the water as if someone is tracing spirals on their skin. The coolish night air comes in through the window, caressing. They lie on the bed drinking the cold beers they'd managed to score before they left town. Plum feels calm and brave. Milagro told her she has a love gift. She says, "Wouldn't you be more comfortable without those?"

He laughs. He gets under the sheet, takes off his wet trunks. She reaches under, puts her hand on him, cradling his balls.

"Is this okay?" He nods.

They lie like that for a long time.

"Do you want me to move my hand?" He shakes his head.

"That could mean two things," and they laugh but Plum doesn't think he wants her to move away or try to get him off because he isn't stirring and she can see a little vein beating at his temple so she kisses it and then whispers, "May I go down?"

He nods but there is some tension in the curve of his lips. Plum stays where she is, kissing

54

his temples and forehead and cheeks, cradling his face in her hand, her other hand on his cock.

She says, "No erections now, whatever you do."

He smiles and his mouth softens. Plum moves down slowly and rests her face against his hip. His groin is flat and smooth. She moves her mouth against him and touches his tip very softly with her lips, then she kisses his shaft and around his groin.

He still isn't responding and he seems a little tense so she comes back up and fits herself into the warm cradle of his arm, her head on his bicep.

That is how they sleep in Milagro's villa, with the beaded glass curtains tinkling in the desert breeze. Deep in the night or is it early morning Plum is lying curved around him, her bare breasts sticking to the breadth of his back, and she finds her hands moving down over his hips and stroking him. He stretches back so that she can touch more. His penis stirs toward her hand and she grasps it. It makes a slapping sound against his flat belly. She moves her hand up and down along the shaft and he sighs softly. She does this for a long time, breathing with him. Then he flips her so she is on top of him with his cock upright in her hand between her legs. He arches his upper back and she keeps going, the skin moving quickly in her palm. He thrusts with his hips and Plum hears him breathing. Sweat pouring off of them. Plum throws back the covers and feels the desert air. She kisses the side of his face to let him know he could keep going as long as he wants even though her hand is starting to cramp. He comes in a huge burst, crying out and gripping her shoulders. She is so relieved that she hardly notices the empty ache between her own legs.

In the morning she opens her eyes in the shadowless flare of light and sees him watching her with the most tender smile all over his face.

"Magic," he says.

She traces her finger along his cheekbone, to his throat, his clavicle. She leans over to kiss him but he pulls away.

"You know, right, Plum, this place is magic?" he says.

"Yes," Then, "You are."

He sits up, drawing the sheet around him. He looks even browner against the white linens. "No, Miss Plum. I'm gay."

She isn't shocked, of course. It's like she's always known. She just hasn't wanted it to be true. He has promised not to go away to school because he loves her. He has come on her belly. It is still sticky there.

"Don't be upset."

"What just happened?"

"I know. I love you. What happened was beautiful. But it's not going to happen again. I didn't mean to hurt you."

She wants to say, but you did hurt me, it's been a year of you hurting me, but she doesn't. Because it isn't really true. He never pretended anything else. Somehow she just didn't want to think, he never kisses me, he wears mascara. What she wants to think is—burning wind, blue pool, neon sign, pink sky, wind chimes, heaving chest, dense muscles, amber skin, avocado sandwich, tango dancers, cutest couple, Villa Milagro. These are the things she wants to hold onto instead.

"Have you been with a guy? "

"No."

"So how do you know?"

"I just do. I've wanted someone so badly. The strange thing is, after what just happened, I'm not afraid now."

Plum thinks about this, isn't quite sure how to take it.

"Not because it wasn't great," he says. "It was so healing. It was like you were comforting me."

She doesn't say anything but she knows that he can see by her eyes that she needs him to comfort her now. He takes her hand and presses his lips to the thin skin. "I'm sorry if I hurt you, Plum."

The love gift, she thinks, is the gift of giving love.

On the drive back they are quiet. The Cadillac doesn't have air conditioning so they leave the windows down and it's too loud to talk much anyway. Plum wants the hot wind to blast her mind, blast away the sand in her throat, obliterate the invisible "S" tattooed on her chest.

"You are going to find him very soon," Plum says, over the wind, after awhile.

This, she is beginning to realize, is her gift.

# Nymph

After she has let War, the skinhead from the Valley, fuck her, he shows her the swastika tattoo on his heavily muscled white thigh. She says, "Do you even know what that is?" trying not to be sick from her hangover and the slashes of blue ink.

He laughs, "It's a fashion statement."

"Have you ever heard of genocide?"

"Why? You a Jew?"

Suddenly she feels as if he can see through her flesh to her organs and bones. She gets up and pulls on her black lace dress. It still stinks of cigarettes and the beer she spilled when he grabbed her to dance with him. Picks up the pointy-toed black satin pumps because her feet hurt too much to wear them.

As soon as she gets home she takes a long hot shower, scrubbing herself everywhere until her skin is bright red, and then she wraps herself in white towels and calls Plum.

Plum is still sleeping in and her voice is hoarse and even softer than usual. They'd been at the gig together and Plum had told her not to go home with anyone who called himself War but she joked it was probably short for Warren and kissed Plum goodbye on the cheek for good luck. There is something charmed about Plum, Sylvie believes. Nothing too bad can happen when she is around.

"But I should have known even your magic doesn't work when I'm alone with Warren and he shows me his swastika tat."

"Oh, God."

"I know. I still feel like vomiting."

"I'm coming over."

While she lies on her bed waiting she spreads her thighs and rubs her clit gently with her knuckle until she feels the tightness and she comes guiltily, counting thirteen contractions. Wonders at how her body can still want this after what it has just been through. But it is the only way she ever feels release.

When Plum gets there they don't talk much, just eat the muffins Plum has brought, watch *Juliet of the Spirits* again and give each other pedicures. She looks at Plum and thinks, what the hell would I ever do without you? They met at a poetry workshop in Venice and fell in love with each other's imagery—blood, lace, booze, angels, emaciated coughing boys. Sylvie's poem—the one about her brother, David, dying and the beautiful nurse—made Plum cry in front of everyone. That was enough to help Sylvie recognize her future best friend. Also they were both shy, their hair was bleached blond then, choppy with dark roots; they only wore black thrift shop dresses or torn Levi's and vintage rhinestone jewelry. The first night they went out together they got drunk in Plum's '65 Mustang on a bottle of Fra Angelica and then slammed in the pit with a bunch of sweating bald boys, stayed up till dawn eating burritos, deconstructing punk rock and trying to figure out why they were attracted to it. After that the friendship was established and the one thing that helped relieve the depressions besides sex. Much better than sex because the times with Plum never backfired. Plum always made her feel better, like holding her grandmother's tiny pink rhinestone chandelier earrings up to the light or watching the sun come up over the city and listening to Iggy and the Stooges in the Mustang.

They know they should stay home tonight but after they've napped and had some take-out sushi and green tea they feel so much better that they decide to go for it. Nothing too hard core though—they'll go to the Odyssey which plays new wave music and has its share of goofs in bandanas and spandex, which can be sort of comforting.

It is always fun to get dressed with Plum because she makes it like a costume ball or something, putting gel in their hair and doing their make-up so they are porcelain pale with dark looming eyes and shiny red lips.

"Let's not wear black tonight," Plum says, but they know that almost everything they have is.

Plum starts rummaging around in the closet and finds some white satin which they'd used once to decorate the apartment for a party. She makes them each a bandeau top and short sarong skirt and they wear the gauze and glitter kids' angel wings they'd bought for Halloween and tossed aside when they decided it was much more punk rock to be she-devils.

The wings have straps that cut into their armpits but they look good, like fairy wings, because of their small size. Plum has some pink, blue and silver glitter in her make-up bag which she uses on their eyelids instead of the dark stuff and when she is through she says, "We're Nymphs, now."

"Nympho-maniacs. At least I am."

"Fine. But just be a choosier one, please."

At the Odyssey, Nymphs turn the color of rainbows. In the strobe lights their wings look as if they are beating, as if the Nymphs will take off into the air. Skinny-hipped boys and metallic girls are gyrating around them, glinting with sweat. The Nymphs dance for a long time without stopping, close together so no one can break into the circle of their energy. It feels like casting a spell.

Later, they sit out on the patio with their cranberry and vodka. When Sylvie tries to get the tiny piece of cocktail napkin out of her ear it sticks so Plum has to help her; they always use the napkins as ear plugs because real rubber ear plugs gross them out and tissue paper is too thin and they both have the irrational fear of losing it down the canal. Even with the napkin ear plugs their ears ring and clang for twenty-four hours afterwards.

The Nymphs look around at the boys with cropped hair and leather jackets, the ones with leopard T-shirts and pointy boots. They all look either too mean or too young or gay.

Plum asks, "What's wrong?" and Sylvie says, "Maybe I should be hanging out somewhere else trying to meet someone. This doesn't look too promising."

"It means a lot to you, doesn't it?" Plum says.

"I can't help it. I'm obsessed. I'm one of those people that never feels whole unless they have their partner. I know not everybody's like that."

Plum's eyes are so big and dark, like compassion spilling up and out. She says, "You're lucky you feel that way. When you find the right person it will be totally amazing."

"I don't feel like I'm ever going to."

Plum looks down at her nervous little hands and takes a breath as if she is about to speak.

"What?"

"I have something I've been wanting to tell you."

She waits. They tell each other everything. Plum never hesitates. It must be bad. Sylvie's mind begins going through a list of bad things—she slept with one of my ex-boyfriends, she doesn't want to hang out with me anymore, she's sick or... "Plum," she says, "you better tell me. I'm starting to get scared."

"I don't want to freak you out. It's nothing horrible, just it might make you uncomfortable." She takes a big gulp of the drink and hands the last sip over.

"We're not uncomfortable about anything with each other."

"I guess that's because I haven't been totally honest. I mean, you might have felt more uncomfortable if you'd known it's this." Plum says, "There's this weird thing. Since I was a teenager. Every one of my friends, after they sleep with me they end up meeting the person of their dreams within a really short time. I can't explain it and I know it sounds like a sick come on but it's the truth."

"Doesn't that hurt your feelings?"

Plum shakes her head. "I've started feeling kind of detached from it in a way. Like, accepting. I might as well use it as a gift."

"I'm flattered you'd want to," Sylvie says. Her face is getting hot and she touches her cheek with the back of her hand. "I mean it's not that."

Plum examines her own hands again. They are so delicate. It is as if the light could shine through them. "You don't have to say anything."

"No. I want to. I'm just shy. I've never..."

Plum nods. "Forget about it," she says. "I must sound like a freak."

"No. But you really are a nymph."

"Like how?"

"Like a woodland sprite. That's what you remind me of. Like a little love goddess or something."

Plum smiles.

"I believe you, Plum."

Plum is beautiful, Sylvie has always thought that. She's even imagined a few times what it would be like to kiss her. It makes so much more sense, somehow, to want to touch this delicate sweet soft person you love, rather than any of the weak boys or the angry boys or the mean boys or the Nazis she'd let inside without even getting to know.

In Plum's stucco bungalow perched in the. Silverlake hills, the moon through the leaves makes the whole room seem to sway. The Nymphs' lips touch, yielding and girlish sweet, no threat the way it always feels with men. Then they are kissing, languidly, liquidly. Plum tastes of the sweet minty things she always keeps in her purse. She takes Sylvie's shoulders and they fall to the bed. Everything soft and silky and their hair flickers and tickles and their skin so petally. Plum takes off her top and then unknots Sylvie's. In all the time they've been friends they have somehow managed not to see each other's breasts. Now

Sylvie knows why, it is because of their hidden fear of this thing that is happening now. Plum's breasts are high and round and the nipples are small and delicate.

Plum starts to untie Sylvie's skirt. She whispers, "Imagine him. He just walked in. He's like a wild animal, so quiet and strong. He's sitting over there. He's unzipping his pants and touching his cock."

"Where?"

"Over there. Hey," Plum whispers into the dark corner. She slips her hand into Sylvie's panties and pulls them gently off her hips. The. way she does it, angling Sylvie so the imaginary boy can see, is like she's showing someone something very precious.

"You're beautiful," Plum whispers. "He thinks so, too. He can't stop staring at you."

She gets off the. bed and kneels in front of Sylvie, pushing apart her thighs with her hands. Sylvie's bareness spread open at the edge of the bed. She can feel the warm night air on her clit and her womb is heavy inside of her. She holds her breasts, the nipples pointing at the boy in the corner. Then she looks at him and he is looking right back at her. He doesn't look away. She loves him. She loves him so much that she wants him to get hard looking at her best friend's slim body. She licks her lips as if she is licking Plum and lets go of her own breasts and pulls Plum's head close.

Plum's tongue teases Sylvie with tiny licks, up and down, then in little circles. Sylvie tries to breathe. Plum puts her hand on her belly and she relaxes a little. She imagines the man in the corner watching them, moistening his hand with his saliva, wetting the shaft of his cock. Plum moves her mouth away and says, "He wishes he was tasting you. You taste so good and sweet." Then she goes back down, pressing her tongue hard and flat this time in steady heavy licks. Sylvie pushes her pelvis up against Plum's mouth and grips with her thighs. There is a fluttering deep in her belly. She keeps moving her legs, spreading them to let Plum in and then gripping again to drive Plum's lips against her. The man in the corner would be aching now, huge. The veins standing out in his neck and arms and in his cock. Sylvie feels it coming. She presses up harder and Plum keeps going. Then it starts, big and deep, a bunch of lush wet blossoms opening in fast motion.

Plum feels so delicate and small in her arms afterwards. Sylvie kisses her mouth, tasting herself, clean, salty, sweet, and they smile at each other in their kiss.

"How do you feel?" Plum asks.

"Great."

"A little weird?"

Sylvie doesn't want to admit.

"It's okay if you do. You know, it wasn't really about us."

"What do you mean?"

Plum draws the sheets up over her breasts. "It was about you and him. That's okay."

Sylvie loves her then, even more, for understanding. "You're still more fun to dance with," she says.

"We'll still be dance partners no matter what happens."

"Thank you, Plum."

Sylvie sleeps more peacefully beside her than she ever has with a man. When they go to the Tropical Bakery the next morning she watches

Plum over the steaming coffee and guava pastries and knows that both of them have silently agreed that what has happened won't ever happen again. But she also knows that it won't hurt the friendship they have. Maybe it makes it stronger.

Two weeks later Sylvie and Plum are doing their first poetry reading at a coffeehouse when Sylvie looks up and sees Ben. His hair is buzzed at the time, and she thinks that is cool and he is wearing canvas high tops which she hadn't been crazy about before—they seemed so lightweight and she preferred hard core combat boots, but after War she has changed her mind. Plus, this guy listens so attentively as she reads and he comes up afterwards and says he thinks she is really talented and he has an openness about him, the way he stands and smiles, and his eyes. Maybe something about him reminds her a little of David, too. Sometimes right when you meet someone you know you are going to sleep with them and that is how it is. She thinks she notices that he has an erection, the beautiful outline of his cock in his jeans. Her panties get wet and her nipples pop out under the thin black silk. She has to cross her legs to quiet the jumping. Later, Sylvie wonders if she would have felt all this if it hadn't been for that night with Plum. You have to believe in magic in order to recognize it.

# *Goddess*

After Coco leaves, Elvis Dean feels like a
magician has put him in a box and sawed
him in half and forgotten the spell to put
him back together again. He doesn't go out with
anyone else. When he's not at work he goes on
runs or stays alone in his bachelor apartment
drinking, listening to old records. writing mono-
logues and watching videos. Months and months
go by and finally his friend Tony drags him out.
"Besides, these ladies are amazing," Tony says.

It is smoky in House of Goddess and Elvis
Dean sits with his friends at a table and drinks
shots of tequila. A girl is dancing on stage and she
has big round breasts, a tiny waist, a round little

ass, long legs. Her hair is long and black to her waist and she has cinnamon skin and huge slanted eyes. In keeping with the goddess theme of the club there is something else about her, too. She is dancing on top of a huge papier mache skull. And she has many arms waving around from her torso. Elvis Dean's friends start talking about her, softly at first, and then louder until they are howling and she is waving her arms like tentacles. Elvis Dean makes a few noises with his friends so they won't give him shit but he knows it sounds strained and fake and he orders another shot.

A second dancer comes out. She is Asian with large wings attached to her back. She dances around as if the wings hurt her. All Elvis Dean can think about—not her perfect body or skin or hair—is that the wings must hurt her. He thinks, fuck, I am dead, my dick is dead, and he wants to go home and drink himself into a coma.

Tony slaps his shoulder and says, "What's up, Deano, she's not doing it for you?" Elvis Dean doesn't know what to say so he just gets up to take a piss. When he comes back he orders another drink and sits down.

This one girl is dancing by herself on the stage now and he looks over and sees she is brown chocolate with golden brown waves of hair and long sinewy legs. Her breasts are high and round under the sheer tunic. She is smiling.

It takes him awhile to realize she is smiling at him. He has another drink. She keeps watching him as she dances, he is pretty sure she is watching, her hands sliding over her breasts and soft belly that indents slightly around her navel, her mouth opening sometimes, her legs wrapping the pole and she is sliding on it and letting her tunic flip up to show off her big firm ass. When she pulls the tunic all the way off he has to take a breath. He wants to plunge into her, into every part of her and never come out.

She comes over to him and takes his hand. Up close, he sees there is something strange about her face. She resembles a cat, almost exactly, the big wide eyes, broad high cheekbones and tiny flat nose.

Her hand is very thin and it feels like a little paw when she takes his. He gulps the rest of his drink and then she takes it and puts it on the table and moves closer to him, her breasts so near he could put his mouth on them. She reaches around and unties her top and pushes her shoulders forward so her breasts swell, then she wiggles slightly and the top comes off in his lap, wet and sparkling. Her nipples are big and dark and succulent, he can't help it, that is the only word for them. Suck suck suck, he thinks. Fuck. His dick feels huge. He shifts in the chair and she leans closer and says. "You like me, baby? You think I got it?" He nods. She says, "You're so sweet, I could tell, not like them, you're so pretty." She touches his hair and the side of his face. She turns slowly around and wiggles her ass for him. He wants to touch it so bad that he has to bite his lip and grip his fingers. She is wearing a G-string, her spread cheeks smooth and brown and welcoming him.

Her hands on the back of a chair, she arches her spine, lifting her ass in the air and waving it from side to side. When she turns around she leans forward, bringing up her shoulders so her breasts push together and swell and she spreads her thighs across his lap and plays with her G-string and then she whispers, "Baby, it's me."

He stares up at her, everything caught in freeze frame. Because he can't believe it. And because he should have known right away.

"I told Tony to bring you," she says. "When he came in I was so relieved. I begged him."

Elvis Dean pulls away from her. "What are you talking about?"

"Help me out of here," she says. "I could never leave. He says the only way we'll get the strength to leave is if we're really in love. And you're the only one."

"Why are you doing this?"

"Baby, it's true. Please. He's dangerous but I haven't been able to get away."

"You're a stripper!" he says. "You're a fucking stripper."

"Please, baby, get me out of here. He's dangerous."

Elvis Dean stands up, pushing her off of him. He looks over to the exit sign above the door. A few steps away.

Coco. It is Coco. He turns back to her strangely changed kitty face. What has happened to her?

He looks to the stage where the woman with the many arms and the winged woman are still dancing. There is a look of terror in them, too. he realizes. The arms and wings look so real.

"Dean."

He reaches for her hand, almost instinctively, dragging her with him through the bar, not looking back, afraid that if he lets himself see her face again he'll stop. Then they are out in the cool night and it was so easy, not the way he'd thought, just the quiet and the neon lights and no one chasing them with knives and guns.

He pulls her toward his car and puts her in, tosses her his jacket, goes around, gets in, too. She puts the jacket over her bare, shivering shoulders. Her long brown legs glow under the dash. Her knees are bony, more fragile looking than he remembers.

"Please, drive."

He does. She huddles against the upholstery, holding herself. After awhile he stops the car and turns to her.

"You better tell me what this is all about."

She clears her throat and fidgets for awhile

but then he grabs her wrists and she settles down and looks at him. He tries not to flinch at the weird change in her face. She is exactly like a huge cat now.

"His name's Wonder. He told me if I came to work for him I'd have everything. And you know how much I wanted to be a dancer, a real one, but he said I'd have everything. Then he said I'd do much better if I had the surgery."

She touches her face. "I didn't know what to do. The other girls all did it. He paid for the whole thing. He said we'd be goddesses."

"House of Goddess," Elvis Dean mutters.

"Yes. He makes us into them. But I didn't think he'd go so far."

"Coco, what the fuck are you telling me?"

"He said we could leave any time but the girls say the only way you can really leave is if someone loves you enough. They say it's like magic, the only thing that works. Otherwise you'll come back. Even if you know he's going to do something terrible."

"Like what?" Elvis Dean really doesn't want her to say.

"You saw us in there," she answers. She removes the metal collar she is wearing, touches her throat and the way she used to do when she didn't want to cry. "I'm so sorry, baby. I'll do anything for you. Can I?"

He turns away from her. "You want me now, huh, so this guy won't turn you into a freak, is that it? Do you know how it's been for me all this time? I've been sick over you, Coco. I haven't been with anyone since you left."

"I'm sorry," she says again.

She reaches to touch his thigh and his muscles tense. But he's hard right away. Wanting her like always.

"Make love with me," she says. "It will break the spell."

"You're a stripper. And you left me."

"I wanted to be a dancer, " she says. "I thought that was the only way and I knew you couldn't understand. I knew I'd hurt you more if I stayed with you and did this."

"Then why did you do it?"

"I was wrong," she says. "I wanted to be a dancer."

And he knows that he never took her seriously before, when he saw how her feet bled and how she'd go to class with bandages on her knees. How she wept when she came home from auditions. When he asked, why do you keep going? she said that the dancing itself was worth everything, even the rejection; it was the only time she was really happy. What about when I make love with you? he had wondered but been afraid to say. And that was why he couldn't take the dancing as seriously as she needed him to, because it made him feel like he didn't matter. Him with his dream of moving to Hollywood to be an actor, (she said there was virtually no dance scene there—not like New York) his classic 70's soul and funk records and his half marathons and his single obsession—her.

"Why did you leave me?"

After Coco danced for Mr. Wonder one afternoon in the reddish dark on the stage at House of Goddess, he told her she had nice technique. He told her that she'd be a great addition to the club. She just needed a little refinement.

What this turned out to mean was that he, Mr. Wonder, Doctor Wonder, would perform cosmetic surgery on her, *gratis*. Not only that, but he would personally care for her until she healed. She would be treated like royalty, and at the end she would look like a superstar, like a diva, a goddess.

She would get to dance, professionally, to be paid—well paid—cared for. She would get free plastic surgery, beauty. There wasn't a lot to think about. Coco already liked how she looked, and other people seemed to, too—especially Elvis Dean—but it hasn't gotten you anywhere, now has it, she told herself. She was still a struggling dancer. Her boyfriend was sweet and lovely but even he didn't take her completely seriously. And all she wanted was to be on a stage worshipped, adored, glimmering like a deity.

That is what Wonder promised her. She had to admit, too, that she had fallen a little under his spell. A tall man with a perfectly proportioned body dressed in expensive suits. Perfect facial features, slicked back black hair. Preternaturally blue eyes and long artistic fingers. He reminded her of a magician.

He would make her into a goddess, into one of the most beautiful women. That is what he promised her. He would make her perfect, and beyond perfect. That is why she went with him.

And the dancing, the dancing is so important—everything. It's like she is walking around as someone else until she dances. Then everybody sees what is really her.

For those things she left her dance classes, her studio apartment in the Village, her boyfriend. It felt like a sacrifice but didn't transcendence always demand that? She'd learned that in ballet class when she was a little girl.

On the day of the surgery she was picked up in a limo. She was told by the driver to relax and she was given some pills to help her do this. The ride through the city at dawn was surreal. The night before, before she took the sleeping pill he gave her, she was sitting up in bed staring at her face in a mirror, remembering the papers she had to sign that protected Wonder from any responsibility, letting her know that there was the very remote chance, but a chance, of death from the anesthesia. But on the way there she felt calm, even blissed out, watching the early morning deliveries, the pigeons scattering, the markets opening, through the window of the limo. She had forgotten about how her face would change.

Wonder nursed her back to health himself. He sat at her side reading her poetry, stroking her, telling her how beautiful she would be, feeding her pills. She felt euphoric and tingling.

But when the bandages came off she saw the cat face and knew what she had done. When she looked at the magician his eyes were like dry ice. So cold they smoked.

"You were already the most beautiful woman in the world," says Elvis Dean when she finishes telling him.

"And now I'm a freak."

"No. You're still a goddess."

She leans back against the seat, slipping one hand down over her breasts, they look glossy like chocolate frosting in the light, over her belly, to the band of her G. Her fingers slide in, forming a V, parting the lips of her pussy so the little ragged fall of petals presses out between. She pokes out her tongue the same way, teasing her upper lip. "Baby," she says. Just the way she used to.

He's angry again now at his helplessness before her. "And now what is it you want? I haven't fucked anyone since you left, Coco. The first time I get a hard on and it's you again! How do you expect. . ."

But he can't finish speaking. He's been alone for so long without her. He thinks of that old wives' tale about how cats can strangle babies, take their breath away. How she will take all of his breath.

How he will let her.

# *Plum*

lum is tired of being alone. She has helped
all her friends find the men or women of
their dreams. At first it was unintentional;
each one just kept falling in love with someone
else after Plum slept with them. Later, she decided not to get attached, just use her gift generous-
ly. But that was in her twenties.

Plum hasn't been with a man in awhile but
then she meets Elvis Dean on the set of a movie
where she is doing costumes. He owns and oper-
ates The Smoothie Theater, a catering truck with
fruit drinks named for famous movie stars, that
goes around to the sets. While she is ordering her
favorite strawberry Marilyn smoothie, Plum stares

at his dark curls, the fullness of his lips, height of his cheekbones, arch of his eyebrows, the pointed tips of his ears, the tiny cross-shaped scar on his left lobe where, he tells her later, it was pierced in the early eighties. His body is lean, intricately muscled, and his skin has a warm goldish glow; he always smells like fresh berries and almonds. Plum finds she is obsessed. She asks him if he is an actor and he shrugs but she presses him and he says, yes, he's done some theater and a beer commercial but this gig is all right in the meantime. When the film wraps he asks her on a date.

Elvis Dean takes Plum for dinner and a movie once a week and holds her hand and calls her sweetie. He always speaks softly to her, and he is beautiful and almost as gentle with her as a girl would be, holding her small face and stroking her long straight black hair. But he never takes off his jeans or touches her breasts or between her legs. Plum's friend Sylvie warns her to be careful, but Plum is so happy to be around Elvis Dean, drinking his strawberry Marilyn smoothies or carob banana Chaplin smoothies and smelling him and feeling the warmth pulsing from the crook of his arm when she nestles there, that she keeps telling herself he is just going slow, he really cares about her and that is why he is waitng, she needs this slowness anyway. Maybe he has something going on of his own, she thinks, some sadness, something he is recovering from. She will be patient.

But one morning at dawn she wakes up wet from a dream. She imagines how she might surprise Elvis Dean, find him all sleepy and relaxed and how she'll crawl into bed with him and stroke his hard muscles and his lean legs and his groin and his cock and how he'll get hard right away without time to think or worry about anything.

The roads are empty and Plum feels wild and free curving through the darkness. Her heart is pounding when she gets to Elvis Dean's apartment. It is still dark out but the sky is starting to glow a little. The air is clear and cold and she can feel her nipples grazing her coat; she is only wearing thigh high stockings and spike heels.

Elvis Dean's door is unlocked and she opens

it and peeks in. He jolts up in bed.

"You scared the fuck out of me," Elvis Dean says as he fumbles for the control to turn off the video that is playing. The video is of Elvis Dean crouching behind a woman, pushing himself into her. The woman is tall, long limbed, feline.

Plum feels her heart sink and the adrenalin start to pump, making her want to run. Here it is again, she thinks. He's going to leave me like all the others. Only this time I don't know if I can handle it. I don't have any more gifts left.

But then something happens. It is as somehow someone else has inhabited her body. Someone bigger and more fierce. That is the only way she can describe it; she has never felt anything like this before. She takes a deep breath and slips inside and shuts the door.

"I'm sorry I scared you," she says. "But I see I've caught you being a very naughty boy."

He seems surprised at her tone. She goes over to him and kneels by the futon. "I think this calls for a spanking."

Elvis Dean's eyes get wide. Then he starts to laugh a little nervously.

"I'm serious," Plum says. "Come here." She sits on a chair.

Elvis Dean stands up and Plum pulls him down over her lap. She pulls his pajama bottoms half way down so his powerful curved ass is up in the air. He starts to laugh again.

"I'm really serious," she says. "I don't like this business of you getting off without me around. I'm going to have to teach you a little lesson."

She slaps his cheek lightly and then again. He doesn't move.

She says, "You don't seem to be feeling this. I'm going to have to do it a little harder."

Elvis Dean doesn't say no, so Plum hits him again and this time his ass jerks up a little and he makes a sound in his throat that is more pleasure than pain so she does it again. She feels him getting hard against her thighs.

"So you like that, huh?" Plum licks her palm and massages the red mark on his ass cheek. She lets her wet fingers slip into the crack. He rubs his groin against her thighs and she smacks him again so the taut flesh moves. He pulls away, sliding down onto his knees.

"What are you doing, bad boy?"

"May I lick your pussy?" he asks.

"What?"

Plum tries to sound indignant but she spreads her legs a little so he can see it naked.

"Say please."

"Please."

She spreads wider. Elvis Dean buries his face between her thighs and she jumps. He slips his tongue into the groove and begins wiggling it around. Plum has to grab onto his hair to steady herself. "So you liked me smacking your ass?" He nods and his tongue moves up and down her clit. He puts his hands on her cheeks and pulls her even closer.

"Well if you're a very good boy..." but then Plum can't talk anymore.

Plum wakes feeling hungover even though she hasn't had anything to drink. What happened? It was like someone else was there with them. There is even a different scent in the air, a shadowy sweetness, not Elvis Dean's, not her own, although she knows it came from her.

"I'm sorry about that," Elvis Dean says.

"It's okay, I'm used to it."

"What do you mean?"

So Plum tells Elvis Dean about how whenever someone has sex with her they find their true love almost immediately afterward.

"I've already found her," Elvis Dean says.

"I can see," says Plum.

"No. That was Coco. After her I was afraid I couldn't perform with anybody else."

"What happened?"

Elvis Dean clears his throat and shakes his head. There is a tightness around his eyes.

"Sweetie?" she says.

"She'd been through a lot of shit," he says, staring at the floor. Then, as if he's awakened from a dream, he looks at her. "She died."

"I'm so sorry."

"It was a long time ago."

Plum lowers her eyes to her breasts that are a lot smaller than the breasts of the woman in the video. "I'm not her," Plum says. "I felt like her before. It's weird, like she was in me or something, but I'm not." Then she says, "I thought I'd accepted that this was the way it was always going to be, but I don't want it to happen with you."

"I'm not going any place," Elvis Dean says.

Plum feel the tears start in her throat, again. "I'm sorry," Plum says. "I wish I was her for you."

"Sweetie! No. You're you. That's all I want."

He moves over and lies heavily on top of her, his cock sliding against her wetness, stirring and big. She reaches down and takes it gently, pressing the tender tip against her opening, then holds still as he pushes up and in. When she yowls he stops rigid and asks if she is okay but in answer she starts moving her hips, driving him deeper against the soft firm wall and his lean muscular abdomen harder against her swelling. There is a hard pressure like all the sadness of lost lovers has gathered between her thighs and he is going to release it, each thrust releasing a little until after a long time her muscles begin helping him, pushing away the sadness out of both of their bodies.

# Fox

Doctor Jacqui Fox has never fallen for a patient in her whole career. So why this one? Good looking, well mannered, soft spoken and probably quite talented. Sensual, sensitive, a bit sad in essence—all good qualities for an actor. Always looks ready to spring or run, she can't tell which. Okay, but should that be enough to start her fantasizing? Most of her patients are couples, older men, or single women. A lot are survivors, like she is. She tries not to assume that because they have these problems they were abused, but it's so common. A lot of them can't face it alone. Even she had to have the therapist bring it up. It took years and it took her stepfather's death. That was when she decided to specialize in sex therapy; before, it was just general counselling. She was uncomfortable sharing those intimacies, saying certain words to her clients, but after the revelation she needed to be as open as possible, like a declaration. You can't keep me imprisoned anymore.

This man wants her help. Erectile difficulties for years, ever since his girlfriend died. Dr. Fox has heard all about her—the story of how he found her again in the strip club. She wonders if he's a bit delusional about the plastic surgery, the goddess thing, this Mr. Wonder. Does some research but can't find anything out about a strip place back east seven years ago. This girlfriend, Coco, the dancer, really had him going, though. Hard. He never seems to have gotten over her death. He still watches videos of them having intercourse—it's the only thing that arouses him. They spend a lot of time on Coco, Dr. Fox and Elvis Dean. It must've been quite devastating. She wonders what it will take to cure him. He won't touch any drugs. "How will I know what I'm really feeling." He's a purist, only wears cotton, eats raw foods, does yoga. Sometimes he looks at her breasts as if they're in his mouth or he'll glance between her legs and that's when she gets wet, just by his eyes. They are dark and glistening, a little slanted, feral. When they met he admitted that part of the reason he'd called was her name. "It was my spirit animal when I was a kid, I found a family in the woods and I'd go visit them." He talks to her about Shakespeare and Charlie Chaplin. He's doing a scene from Hamlet in his acting class. They talk about James Dean—that is her patient's real last name—and how he thinks no one will ever be that again although they all try. She tells him he has something of that quality—that sulking tough vulnerability, hardness barely diguising sweetness. They talk about sex, his sex with Coco, and this is what makes her body wake.

The fantasy is based on the first time he came to see her.

The red light goes on in her office and she goes to meet him in the lobby. He is tan and muscular, wearing soft, faded khakis and a light blue vintage short sleeved shirt. He follows her into the office and she sits down, crosses her legs, asks him how he is.

He shifts on the couch. "I'm pretty good, a little nervous but good."

"Why are you nervous, do you think?"

"I've never done this before."

"Do new things usually make you nervous? "

His mouth twists wryly. "Sometimes."

"Is it difficult for you to talk about your feelings?" she asks.

"I keep quiet usually," he says.

"And why is that?"

"You don't know who to trust always."

She leans closer, almost imperceptibly and furrows her brow very slightly. "Have you had problems with people not being trustworthy?"

"Sometimes. A little. Not too bad."

"But sometimes, yes?"

"Yes. I guess."

She unfolds her palms and rests them on her slender thighs. "I hope you feel you can trust me. This is all confidential and I want you to be at ease."

"Uh huh," he says. He doesn't sound so sure. In fact it sounds like there is a question mark at the end of his answer.

"Why are you here?"

"I've been having some performance anxiety about sex."

"That's very common with men. Are you involved with anyone?"

"No. It's been a long time."

That was the real session. She remembers every word. Then she adds some.

"I'm going to be talking to you pretty directly about sex, is that all right?"

He nods.

"How do you feel about it?"

He doesn't answer. His eyes have a burning look.

"Is that a hard question for you to answer?" She emphasizes the word hard.

"Yes," he says.

"This may be difficult but I believe it will be helpful. Would you like to see my nipples now?"

Elvis Dean tries not to laugh. Dr. Fox thinks

she can detect something going on in his pants.

"Does this embarrass you?"

"Yes, a little."

"Do you like the idea of my nipples?" she says softly, moving her hands lightly over her thighs.

He nods.

"May I show you?" Dr. Fox asks, moving her hands up to her hips.

Nods again.

Dr. Fox slowly moves her fingers up her torso to her breasts. They feel swollen, like they are going to pop out on their own. The thought of him sitting there looking at them makes her sizzle between her thighs. She unbuttons her suit jacket and takes it off. Then she unbuttons her blouse very slowly. Her breasts are straining her bra. She pushes it down so her nipples show, grazing the top of the satin.

"My nipples feel very aroused and sensitive, looking at you," she says.

He is staring at her breasts. She knows he is hard.

"How do you feel now?" she asks.

He shrugs. He reminds her of a little boy spying on a woman through a hole in a wall.

"Do you feel aroused?" she asks.

He smiles shyly. She licks her palm and massages her nipples.

"I'd like for you to tell me about some sexual practice you enjoy," she says. "Do you like to kiss?"

He nods, still staring at her breasts.

She licks her lips. "What else? You have a wonderful mouth, by the way. Do you like to look?"

Elvis Dean nods again. Dr. Fox pulls up her skirt and uncrosses her legs. She slips two fingers down and parts the lips. "Did you know that the penis and the clitoris are the same type of tissue?" she says.

Her breath gets faster.

"Did that shock you, seeing my pussy?"

"No," he says. He sounds very strong, not shy at all.

"I'm quite wet," she says. "Just from looking at you. You're a beautiful man. You are also a very sensitive man, but strong. Women and men must get very aroused by you all the time."

Elvis Dean blushes.

"I'm sorry to embarrass you. Can you tell me how you feel?"

"Slightly uncomfortable."

"Do you feel aroused?"

"Yes."

"Is your penis hard now?"

"Yes."

"Do you like to masturbate?"

"Yes."

"Do you masturbate often?"

"Yes."

"Does it soothe your pain?"

"Sometimes. Sometimes it makes me forget what is bothering me and sometimes it makes things hurt more."

"I think it would be good for me to see you masturbate and for you to masturbate in front of me so it is less isolating."

Elvis Dean looks like he is going to get up and bolt but he doesn't.

"Does that make you uncomfortable?" she asks.

"Yes."

"I don't want you to be uncomfortable. But I would like it if you could put one hand on your penis."

Elvis Dean does it with an assertion and calm that Dr. Fox has never seen from him. She has to grip her thighs together to quiet the stirring in her clitoris.

"Very good," she says. She moves her legs apart again. "Elvis Dean, I'd like you to unzip your pants and stroke your penis, please."

She goes over to him.

"May I kiss you?"

He nods and she leans down and takes his face in her hands. The cheekbones feel small and sharp. It is like holding the face of a beautiful animal. She presses her lips against his and feels a jolt go through her body. He takes his cock out and rubs it while she licks his mouth, bites his lips and whispers into him.

"I think you are doing very very well, Elvis Dean. You are going to be able to express yourself exactly as you choose. You are going to be totally fulfilled."

She spreads her legs and sits on his lap. He

keeps jerking his hand up and down and bouncing her on his taut thighs. She rips open his shirt and slides her hand over the hard plane of his chest.

"You have a penis as beautiful as the rest of you," she says.

When he comes Dr. Fox feels it like her own. The warm liquid spills tenderly onto her thighs and his whole body falls heavily against her. She strokes his curly head and whispers into her ear.

"Yes. Elvis Dean. I'm so glad you came. I don't know if you need me anymore. But I like you so much I think you'll have to come back and see me next week. No charge."

This is the fantasy. What is remarkable about it is that it makes her come. Although she is an expert at helping other people get in touch with their orgasms she hasn't had one in a long time, since she split up with Ian. Elvis Dean makes her come.

"I met someone," he tells her.

She tries to maintain the same calm composure as always.

"Yes."

"Well, I mean, I've known her now for awhile, I might have even mentioned her. The designer. From work."

Dr. Fox nods. "Yes, Plum."

"You remember everything."

"That's my job."

"Well we made love," he says. His face is shining. He looks very young.

"Really. And how do you feel?" She doesn't have to ask; it's obvious.

"Great. I feel great. I feel like the spell's been broken."

Why does this hurt her? She should be happy for him, both of them. The girlfriend's been waiting for months now.

Elvis Dean wants to tell her every detail and she has to listen because that is what she does. Listen. While they tell her. She is horrified at herself, at her desire for him. especially at the self-hatred that's coming up, what she's helped people fend off for themselves for years. It's as if it all accumulated in her and now she's using it. Old. Wrinkled. Perverted.

But he adds, "You helped me so much. I think you are a gorgeous, brilliant woman. I couldn't have done it without you."

"Thank you," she says.

"I wanted to know if it would be okay if I told you something."

"Of course, Dean."

"I've been fantasizing about you. I imagine this one thing." He recounts almost word for word the fantasy she has about him. Even how she's sitting, her panties, the things she says.

"That is extraordinary."

"Really? I thought it was pretty basic. It must happen to you all the time."

"No. Especially not this way," she says. "Believe me."

"Well, thank you. It was always very real. It helped me."

"Thank you," she says when he leaves. "I must tell you though, I don't think I can be seeing you anymore."

When he asks her to explain she tells him. "I believe you're going to be very fulfilled now, Dean. You won't need me. Besides, I have some personal conflicts that I foresee arising. I can recommend someone of course, if you'd like."

He nods and doesn't press her. She wishes she could thank him for helping her come again. When he leaves she takes off her panties and spreads her legs in the leather chair where he was sitting. She can still feel the warmth of his seat, sense his scent in the room, hear his voice in her head saying she is gorgeous, brilliant. She imagines him making love to a slender lovely young woman whose heart has broken more times than Dr. Fox's heart has been broken and who is for the first time, no longer afraid. Tears come, but Jacqui Fox does too.

# *Change*

Carmelita is jealous of every pretty woman she sees. She keeps imagining them with her boyfriend, Tony.

In school she is reading Ovid and she wishes that, like the women in the myths, she could be changed by her feelings into something else. If she can't change into another more beautiful woman, she would like to at least be a tree, or a flower, a fountain or an animal, so that she wouldn't have to think of any of this anymore.

Carmelita is the middle sister in a family of five. All of the sisters have long shiny hair and brown skin and big brown eyes and full lips. They are all smart and stylish and athletic and talented.

Carmelita is no exception except that she doesn't feel that she is any of these things. None of the other sisters seem to have this problem. Carmelita thinks this is because they are more good looking and smarter, etc. than she is but really this isn't true. It is just that somehow Carmelita got lost. Her oldest sister is the oldest and her youngest is the baby. Her second sister is in medical school and the fourth sister is blond. Her mother has told her that they were sure Carmelita was going to be a boy. She knows that her parents, especially her father, were disappointed. Her blond-haired sister's blond hair made them forget their disappointment and the youngest was a surprise so no one was hoping for boys anymore. Maybe this is why Carmelita wishes she was different, she's not sure.

She's had a series of boyfriends but she's never been in love until Tony. He is a trainer at the gym where she teaches step aerobics and he's also trying to pursue a career in song writing. Beautiful big muscles and a soft Bronx accent, dark green eyes with long eyelashes and thick brown hair. Sometimes before they started dating he'd watch her teach and she'd feel him like a bolt of energy making her start to pound. The sweat poured down and her crotch throbbed and it was like they were making love. In the locker room she peeled off her shorts and wondered if he'd been able to detect the swelling of her vulva under the thin shiny fabric. At this time she forgot to compare herself to the other women and maybe that is one reason why she wanted him so much.

Tony makes her laugh. He gives her piggy back rides and orders a lot more food than she would normally get—pizza, falafel, samosas— and tells her he gets a hard on watching her eat it. He rubs the soft slight swell of her belly and tells her how sexy it is and that he likes her ass; he buries his face in it and moans and kisses it and grabs it and she starts liking it more. When he sees the picture of her family he doesn't comment on how beautiful all the sisters are or seem stunned by them as most people do; he just smiles politely, hands the picture back to her and gently rummages between her thighs with his warm hand. When he makes love to her it is rough and sweet at the same time. He talks to her in his low, rumbling voice, telling her how great she is, how pretty, how much he loves to be inside her. Sometimes he sings softly to her, sentimental love songs. He grabs her so hard that she feels the bulge of all his muscles and the heavy weight of him and she wants to just be crushed there and wake up in the morning changed like in the mythology.

So why is she afraid? She realizes that love doesn't magically make everything change, that transformation isn't so easy. She begins to wish that she could be a tree or a flower or an animal if she cannot be the most beautiful woman.

In the fantasy, Tony is a contestant on a TV show. Three women are behind a screen answering questions for him. One has short platinum hair, small childlike features and gigantic breasts, one is dark with sleek black hair in a ponytail and a big perfect ass and one has impossibly narrow hips, long colt-like legs and cascades of brown hair. When Tony asks them to describe their best feature the one with the ass turns around and wiggles it, lifting up her skirt, the one with the legs spreads them and the one with the breasts blithely removes her halter top. The screams of the audience are enough of an answer for Tony. Then he asks the women to describe each other's best features to him. One sucks the other's nipple and one licks the other's pussy in response. They make pleasure noises. By the end of the questions most of their clothes are removed. Tony chooses the one with the long legs but he gets to see the other two first when they come out to meet him. The blond is still topless and Tony gets a huge hard on when he sees her. She kisses him, pressing her bare tits against his chest. He moans softly and looks like he is going to cry as she walks away from him. The dark woman flashes her ass at him and he clutches her big cheeks in the G-string under her skirt when she turns around and kisses him with her full swollen-looking lips. Tony's dick gets bigger in his pants. Carmelita usually comes when the long-legged woman walks out and Tony puts his arm around her and she pulls her panties away so he can see her pussy. Then Carmelita cries herself to sleep. She tries to put herself in the fantasy but it never works. The women always come back in. Where am I, she wonders?

There are a lot of fantasies like this one. Every time they go out and see a beautiful woman Carmelita gets a painful twinge in her chest and between her legs. She knows that she will go home and while Tony is making love to her with his hot thick jolting cock she will wonder if he is thinking of the woman and this will make it impossible for her to come. After he leaves she will be distracted and tense and still swollen and later that day she will slide her fingers between the lips of her pussy and fondle and rub herself thinking about the woman she saw the night before. This will always make her come and it will always make her cry. After awhile this happens even when Tony isn't there. She will see a woman when she is by herself and feel the same painful twinge, imagining Tony's response, and then she will have to go masturbate. It becomes more and more urgent, more and more intense when she comes. It makes her want Tony more than ever but when she is with him she thinks of the women and can't come.

The women are of every different race and

type. They have long shiny hair or wild curly hair, peachy skin or bronze skin or shiny ebony skin; they almost all have big breasts—bigger than Carmelita's, longer legs and more pronounced, jutting features. Carmelita knows that Tony loves her, loves the way she looks, and who she is. She knows that surface beauty is only superficial, of course she knows this. But the feelings won't go away. The pain becomes more than a twinge; it's like an electric shock. The more powerful the shock at seeing the beautiful woman means the more powerful orgasm Carmelita will have, alone, without Tony.

Does she desire the women? No. She wishes she did. It might make the whole thing easier, less painful. She sometimes idealizes lesbians, like her friends Marnie and Dani, thinks they have a better time communicating, thinks they are less jealous, more sensitive to each other's feelings. But if she were gay, she would have made that choice awhile ago. It would have differentiated her from her sisters and given her some kind of identity and maybe she would be happier. But she loves men. Not only their cocks but their smells and smiles and laughs and density and breadth and hardness and hoarseness. And she loves Tony. She loves him and she wants him to get to fuck all the beautiful women in the world and she feels as if she would die if he did and she wishes she could change into all the most beautiful women in the world for him, a different one every night so he would never get bored.

She knows this is unhealthy and she doesn't share it with Tony, who she knows would be very upset and also comforting but who couldn't take the pain away. She goes to a shrink who is helpful briefly but then states, "Well, let's just get it out there, you aren't the most beautiful woman in the world." This is not particularly helpful as a dose of reality because Carmelita is already acutely aware of the fact. She tunes out and hardly hears how the therapist goes on to say that still, Carmelita is nice-looking and a nice person and Tony obvious-ly is in love with her so she shouldn't be upset.

Carmelita feels that somewhere deep inside she is the most beautiful woman in the world, that her love makes her that, but that no one, not even Tony, can see it, and that this is one of the things that hurts her so much. Tony plays Frank Sinatra and when the song, "The Most Beautiful Girl," comes on, he doesn't sing it to her like he does with the other songs. She feels it embarrasses him a little. That he can't say she is the most beautiful girl because he knows it isn't really true and he doesn't want to sound dishonest or phony.

Carmelita and Tony are talking after they've made love and he tells her that he is in a twelve step program. Carmelita isn't surprised—a lot of people she knows are, and she noticed that Tony never drinks. It makes her feel closer to him, that he's told her, and she tells him that she is proud of anyone who can do that—Tony's been sober for ten years. Carmelita thinks her fantasies are an addiction—she can't stop them and they make her feel worse. She asks Tony what helps him besides meetings.

"I write my feelings down in a journal," Tony says, "You should try it. It's really great how it works."

Carmelita used to keep a journal as a teenager. She even dreamed of being a writer then. Usually the things she wrote weren't just what happened to her; she liked to embellish them with surreal, metaphoric imagery. If she was jealous, for instance, she would write about a girl whose face turned green and who ended up running away to live in an arboretum disguised as a plant. Or if she was angry she wrote about a girl who spontaneously combusted. Carmelita began to think that the stories were too weird so she stopped writing them.

But this thing Tony says makes her reconsider. So she buys a journal—it's actually an artist's sketch book with a thick black binding—and she starts writing things down. The only thing she really wants to write down, though, the most interesting part of her life, are the fantasies. She gets so wet when she's doing it that she thinks she'll soak right through to the chair. Sometimes she has to stop to get off in the middle, bucking at her desk. When Carmelita writes the fantasies in her journal she doesn't cry. Afterwards she feels stronger. She reads them to herself and masturbates after she can't come with Tony.

One night Tony comes over and takes Carmelita into the city for Italian food. They eat

pasta and veal and drink red wine and through
the whole dinner Tony watches her and touches
her and once while she is sucking her linguini he
puts her hand on his dick to show her how hard
he is. Carmelita looks up and sees a model she
recognizes from all the fashion magazines walk
into the room. She looks supernatural with her
glowing skin, her long legs, her almost animal
features. She is wearing a tank top without a bra
and her breasts are big with erect nipples under
the cotton. She is with a very handsome man but
Carmelita hardly notices him. The food suddenly
cramps in her gut and she feels like she can't swal-
low. Instead of getting up and running to the
ladies room to recover though, Carmelita thinks,
I will write a story about a girl who sees the
model her boyfriend is obsessed with in a restau-
rant. The girl will proposition the model and the
model will come home with them and fuck the
boyfriend while the girl watches. When Carmelita
thinks this she realizes that she is wet and she
takes Tony's hand under the table—he's just
glanced at the model—and dips his fingers into
her tiny black lace panties. He breathes in the

scent and licks his fingers. He looks at Carmelita and not at the model when he does this. He doesn't even mention the model even though she is so famous that everyone in the place is scrambling.

They leave soon after that and walk through the city. It is hot and steamy. They smell spicy food, garbage and rotting flowers. Carmelita can also smell the scent of her own sex on Tony's hands mixed with the scent of garlic and wine. Everything is lit up with a blurry glow—the little Korean markets with the fruit out in front, the glass facades of restaurants full of people, the many many beautiful people. Carmelita realizes she has kept a little mental log of all the beautiful women she has seen since she met Tony and that she could list them all off in perfect detail—everything they wore, everything about them.

They take the train back to Brooklyn and Tony starts undressing her in the elevator of the brownstone, running his hands up her thighs and pulling off her panties, helping her step out of them so her high heels don't get caught, tucking them in his pocket, lifting her breasts out of her bra under her dress. He takes his thumb knuckle and slides it against her swollen clitoris which is exposed now under the dress.

In his apartment he starts to kiss her. He tastes of meat and wine and she can feel the thickness of his muscles and of his cock. His fingers move playfully between her legs, curling her hair, spreading her lips, caressing the full center. He takes off his jeans and she helps his cock out of his shorts. While she strokes him she starts talk-ing—"Did you see that woman in the restau-rant?" she says. Tony opens his eyes and looks at her to make sure it's okay but she finds that she is smiling. She's the girl in the story. "What if she was here? Her breasts were so big, heavy and big but she was so slender. They'd feel so full falling against her delicate rib cage. And her legs were so long. If she spread them they'd go off the bed." Tony lets her stroke him but he seems nervous. "Don't worry, baby," she says. "I want you to think about them. Like remember that girl at the beach with the long braids and the bikini? What about sliding sun tan oil on her legs and her ass, spreading her cheeks and slipping your hand into her ass. And that girl on the train last month in the really short baby blue skirt. You could have put your hands up her skirt and ripped off her panties so easily. She probably smelled smoky and sweet and her panties with that little bit of cream on them from the feel of your hands."

She goes on like this while he gets bigger in her hand and then she climbs up on top of him and spreads herself and slides down. Her body clenches like a fist around him, drawing him deeper in. She's not talking anymore. She is infused with all of them, with their beauty, with their power, with their wholeness. None of them broken the way she is. It is like in the stories, she feels, the myths of transformation. She will not be a flower or an animal or a tree or a fountain like the woman who cried herself into one. She will rise up, wholly herself.

## About the Author

Francesca Lia Block lives in Los Angeles.

## *About The Publisher*

Circlet Press was founded in 1992 to publish works that were not finding homes in mainstream publishing because they combined the erotic with the fantastic. Since then, Circlet has published over thirty anthologies, short story collections, and novels, all pushing the envelope of what is possible with fantastic fiction and erotic fiction. Numerous stories that first saw print with Circlet have been selected for inclusion in *Best American Erotica* and other annual collections, and Circlet titles are perennial nominees in the Lambda Literary Awards and Firecracker Alternative Book Awards.

If you would like to know more about Circlet Press, please visit our home on the World Wide Web at www.circlet.com or write for our catalog.

- sequined head bands
- cats in hats photo shoot
- Rite Aid develop photos
- cat hair          (poloroid steal)